This Little Tiger book belongs to:

_____

_____

_____

For Georgia, Isabel and Victoria
~ *J.S.*

For Jane – howdy pardner!
~ *T.W.*

LITTLE TIGER PRESS
An imprint of Magi Publications
1 The Coda Centre, 189 Munster Road, London SW6 6AW
www.littletigerpress.com

First published in Great Britain 2004
This paperback edition published 2007

ISBN 978-1-84506-673-4

A CIP catalogue record for this book
is available from the British Library.

Printed in China
2 4 6 8 10 9 7 5 3 1

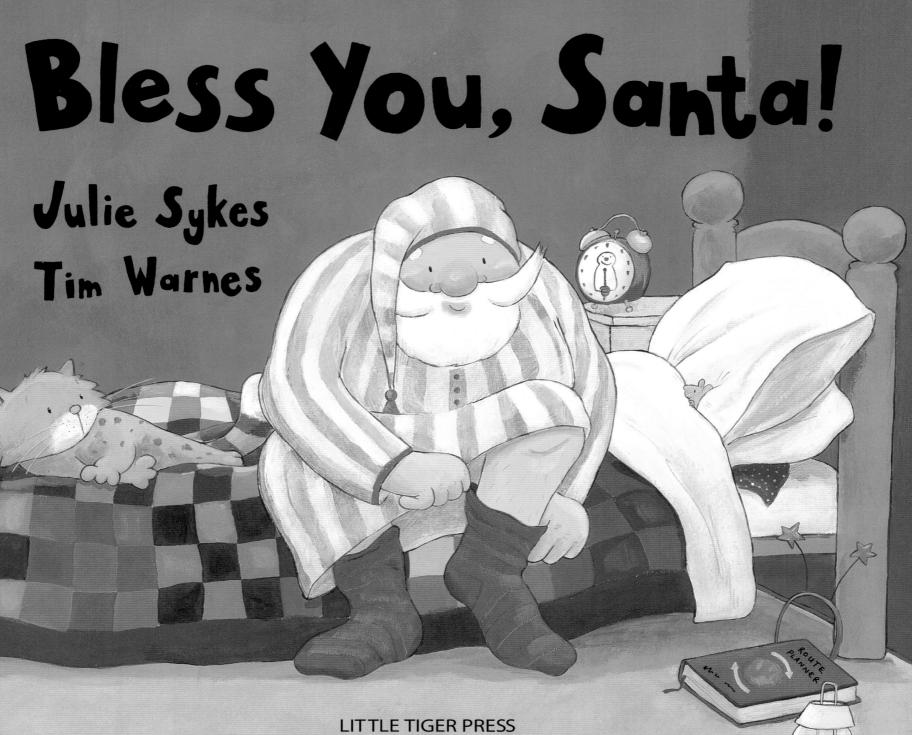

Bless You, Santa!

Julie Sykes
Tim Warnes

LITTLE TIGER PRESS

London

It was almost Christmas and Santa
was up early.

"Jingle bells, jingle bells," he sang
cheerfully. "Breakfast first and then to work."

He made the coffee and toast, but as
he poured cereal into his bowl, Santa's nose
began to tickle.

"*Aah, aah, AAH . . .*

DECEMBER
23

"ACHOO!"

he roared. His sneeze blew cereal all over the place.

"Bless you, Santa," said Santa's cat, shaking cereal out of her tail. "That's a nasty cold."
"Oh no!" said Santa in alarm. "It can't be! It's nearly Christmas. I don't have time for a cold!"

After breakfast Santa rushed to his workshop
and got to work on the unfinished toys. Merrily
he sang as he painted a robot. But Santa's sneezes
were growing larger and louder.

"Aah, aah, AAH...

"ACHOO!"

"Bless you, Santa," squeaked Santa's little mouse, gathering the beads his sneeze had scattered.

"Bless you, Santa," said Santa's cat, chasing paper stars as they fluttered around. "You sound awful. Go and sit by the fire."

"I feel awful!" snuffled Santa. "But I can't rest yet. It's nearly Christmas, and I have to finish these toys or there will be no presents for all the . . . *Aah, aah, AAH* . . .

"ACHOO!"

Santa sneezed so hard that he slipped over and landed in a stack of balls. Down the balls tumbled, bouncing off Santa and bopping around the room. They crashed into cars, they pushed over paint pots, they toppled the teddy bears and *ruined* the rockets.

"ACHOO!"

"Just look at this terrible mess!"
wailed Santa. "I'll never be ready
in time for Christmas now!"

"Go to bed, Santa," ordered his little mouse. "You're not well. Your nose is so red the reindeer could use it to guide your sleigh! We'll clean up this mess and get everything ready for Christmas."

So Santa's mouse put Santa
back to bed with a mug of hot milk
and a little medicine to help his cold.
Santa snuggled under his quilt.
He sneezed . . .

"A C H O O !"

He sniffled . . .

And finally he snored.

Meanwhile, back in the workshop,
Santa's friends worked as hard as they
could. They mopped . . .

They repaired . . .

They glued . . .

They snipped, they stuck, and they wrapped.
Faster and faster they worked until every
single present was finished. Then sleepily
they stumbled to bed.

The next evening, as the sun set, the animals waited with the sleigh piled high with toys.

"Where is Santa?" asked Santa's cat. "I hope he's better!"

"Who's going to drive the sleigh and deliver all the presents?" asked the reindeer.

"Listen," said Santa's cat. "Can you hear something?"

The animals listened.

"It's Santa!" squeaked Santa's little mouse. "Are you better, Santa? Can you deliver the presents?"

Santa wrinkled his nose. *"Aah, aah, AAH . . .*

"Only kidding! I feel much better. Bless you, everyone. You did a great job! Thanks to you all, I will get these presents delivered in time for Christmas day."

Santa climbed aboard his sleigh. "Reindeer, up, up, and AWAY!" he shouted.

It was a busy night as Santa flew
around the world delivering presents.

When at last Santa landed back at the North Pole, the sun was rising. But he hadn't finished yet.

"These presents are for you," said Santa.

"Presents for us!" squealed Santa's cat.

"Th . . . Th . . . THAA . . .

"A C H O O !"

Santa's cat sneezed so hard that a pile of
snow fell off the trees and buried everyone.
"Bless you!" laughed Santa. "And
Merry Christmas to you, too!"